YOU CAN BET ON THAT

THINK YOU CAN HANDLE
JAMIE KELLY'S FIRST YEAR OF DIARIES?

AND DON'T MISS . . .

DEAR DUMB DIARY,

YEAR

TWO

YOU CAN BET ON THAT

BY JAMIE KELLY

SCHOLASTIC INC.

ISBN 978-0-545-64257-6

Copyright © 2014 by Jim Benton

All rights reserved. Published by Scholastic Inc.
SCHOLASTIC and associated logos are trademarks and/or registered trademarks of Scholastic Inc.
DEAR DUMB DIARY is a registered trademark of Jim Benton.

12 11 10 9 8 7 6 5 4 3 2 1   14 15 16 17 18/0
Printed in the U.S.A.   40
First printing, June 2014

*Special thanks to Kristen LeClerc,
Shannon Penney, Abby McAden,
Jackie Hornberger, and Yaffa Jaskoll.*

THIS DIARY IS THE PROPERTY OF:

Jamie Kelly

SCHOOL: <u>Mackerel Middle School</u>

PERCENTAGE OF NICENESS: <u>REASONABLY NICE</u>

PERCENTAGE OF MEANNESS: <u>NORMAL AMOUNT</u>

LOOK I'M PLENTY NICE. THE PERFECT AMOUNT. NOT A CRAZY AMOUNT OR ANYTHING.

I'M PLENTY NICE.

I'LL BET

that you think it's okay to look at somebody else's

DIARY....

Dear Whoever Is Reading My Dumb Diary,

You're really kind of gambling with your life here, you know, reading somebody else's private — yet **highly important** — diary. **I'll bet** you're the type of person who would sell your mom for a donut, and you don't even really like donuts much, which makes it way worse than if you were super into donuts. I mean, if you're going to sell your mom, you should at least do it for something you **like**.

So put the diary down, you rat, and back away from the table before you lose something more than just a bet. (I'm pulling my finger across my neck in a threatening way right now.)

Signed,

Jamie Kelly

P.S. If you don't like donuts, you might like muffins or cupcakes, which are just muffins in **clown makeup**.

P.P.S. Wait. Why am I helping you sell your mom?

SUNDAY 01

Dear Dumb Diary,

The Internet is one of the most sophisticated pieces of human engineering **ever**. It was designed to help people all over the world share pictures of cats and lie to each other.

Here's a handy checklist to help you tell if somebody on the Internet is lying to you:

1.) They write you an email.
2.) That's it.

They write you an email. **That's how you can tell.**

It will be an email from somebody you don't know and will say you've won a prize or inherited money, or there's something wrong with your computer/account/internal organs and they need all your private information to fix it. It makes me wonder what all the crooks were doing while they were **waiting** for the Internet to be invented.

We talk about Internet stuff like this often because everybody is using it more and more at my school. I think that's a good thing, but I dimly remember that there used to be human beings that we called "librarians," and I have this nagging feeling they did important stuff with things we called "boks" or "boacks" or something like that, before the Internet did everything for us.

Maybe I'm just imagining them.

Oh well.

You might remember, DD, that Isabella and I and this one blond girl are now all founding members of the Student Awareness Committee. So we have a little blog on the Internet that we started to make other students aware of things, I guess. I don't know. This was the blond's idea.

Personally, I don't really like **being aware** of things. It makes it harder to ignore them.

Sunday used to be the day I reserved for doing the homework I should have done Friday night or Saturday morning or Saturday afternoon or Saturday night, but these days I spend a lot of Sunday hiding from my mom, who has decided that she wants to **make me clothes**.

Let's just pause and take a deep breath and contemplate the staggering impact of what I just said.

Back when she was a little girl, making your own clothing was probably a **great** idea. Her mom and the lady who harvested coal or whatever would take a covered wagon over to where they were planning on signing the Declaration of Independence one day, and they would make their daughters clothes.

But not anymore, Mom. **Not anymore.**

my mom used to make clothes while she watched Julius Caesar Live on a steam-powered T.V.

So far, Mom has only made a couple of things, but the day will come when she expects me to wear one of them outside the house. I am a very optimistic person, and I'm hoping that all of humanity will have been destroyed in a **massive flaming meteor strike** by then.

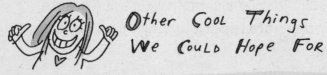

Other Cool Things We Could Hope For

Earth cracks in half

with people on one side and Mom's homemade clothes on the Other

GNASH GNAW GNAW

Zombies that crave sewing machines instead of BRAINS Attack only my HOUSE

Mom goes insane and thinks threads are SNAKES

Is that too mean? It's not too mean. Seriously. You don't have to wear her creations.

MONDAY 02

Dear Dumb Diary,

Today, my social studies teacher, Mr. Smith (who wears a wig), announced that we're going to be doing a section on debate. Debate is when you argue with somebody, but you aren't allowed to call them ugly just because you're losing, which is weird because that would be the **perfect time**.

In the past, we've had debate sections in English, but since everybody argues about everything these days, debate is getting super-popular.

And I guess we need to learn debating skills in case we ever have a disagreement with somebody who is **very attractive**, and we can't come up with anything to say that will hurt their feelings during the argument.

without debate, Arguing with a perfectly cute bunny might be IMPOSSIBLE

I 2 KEWT

But I believe that nature is beautiful and perfectly balanced, and therefore there's SOMETHING gross and ugly about everybody that you can haul out and criticize. Further proof of how optimistic I am, I suppose.

This is why I asked Angeline if she wanted to be my opponent. This, and the fact that if we partnered up with each other, there would be no risk of either one of us having to face off with Isabella.

I'm not that thrilled about partnering with Angeline, but when you **face off** with Isabella, she might actually try to **take your face off**.

Before we actually have the debates, we have to learn **THE BIG OFFICIAL RULES OF DEBATE**. Mr. Smith began listing them today.

Like, if you make a statement, you have to give factual proof.

And you may not throw things at your opponent. (He was looking right at Isabella when he said that rule.)

And you must remain calm and may not call names. (Again, looking at Isabella.)

And you may not threaten your opponent, either during class or later, at night, over the phone with a fake voice and the sound of a chainsaw in the background. (Isabella again. Seriously, I think almost all of the **rules of debate** were made for Isabella.)

The winner of each debate gets to pick the debate topic for the next team. Mr. Smith says that way we won't be able to prepare our arguments — we'll have to debate using only our **wits**, the way wild animals do.

Wait. Wait. Let's debate about this.

Isabella partnered up with Dicky Flartsnutt. You might remember, Dumb Diary, that Dicky is kind of a friend of ours, even though he will never let you totally forget that he was **BORN TO NERD.**

Dicky is very sweet, but he's sort of like a baby goat chained to a tree in a pit full of tigers with a bunch of cinnamon buns tied to him. (It's a well-known science fact that tigers love cinnamon buns, probably.)

We've become attached to Dicky and we feel a bit protective of him. None of us would **ever** do anything to hurt his feelings in a million years, which says a lot, because in most cases, Isabella would be willing to hurt most people's feelings **for** a million years.

Actually, I don't think Dicky could even handle the baby goat.

I'm sure Angeline will put something up on our Student Awareness Committee blog about the debate project. And I'm sure it will be **very chirpy and perky**, like all her posts.

One time, she actually posted about how much **fun** it was to post on the blog. And then she put up pictures of herself doing it.

And she posted about how much **fun** it was to put up the pictures.

And then she posted about how much **fun** it was to post about how much **fun** it was to put up the pictures, too.

Angeline, the Internet only **APPEARS** to be interested in what you're saying because it can't stand up and walk away while you're talking to it.

IF I'm being perfectly honest here, I'm a little tired of the cat pictures.

And we don't need to see photos of your meals, either.

INTERNET

TUESDAY 03

Dear Dumb Diary,

Diseases.

That's what Mrs. Curie, my science teacher, wanted to talk about today.

I learned that very few diseases are appealing, and that you can protect yourself from a ton of them just by washing your hands.

Hand sanitizer attacks 98% of all germs, and 100% of all paper cuts and hangnails. I think it's designed that way so that when you start violently shaking your hands in pain, the dead germs go flying off. Live germs all over your hands are only **slightly worse** than dead germs all over your hands.

Paper cuts are so painful they should use paper as martial arts weapons.

At first, this might make you think that sanitizer scientists are pretty clever, but remember, these scientists are still totally cool with **not** killing 2% of the germs on your hands. That's about **ONE MILLION GERMS**, who are now full of alcohol, staggering around on your hands, super-angry that you wiped out their families and tried to kill them, too.

Do we want this? Vengeful, incoherent germs plotting against us?

Scientists: **Think. Things. Through.**

Isabella seemed interested in what Mrs. Curie was saying, but I'm sure she was just curious about whether there were any minor diseases that could be slipped into her mean older brothers' cornflakes undetected. Isabella is very sweet and would only want her brothers to have **minor** diseases. But she did ask if any germs were smart enough to be trained, like **attack dogs**.

Angeline was perky and attentive throughout the disease discussion, and it occurred to me how different the three of us are:

for example,
I am **NORMAL**.

But Angeline is
ABNORMAL.

And Isabella is
ABNORMALLER.

After class, Angeline started bugging us to contribute something to the Student Awareness Committee blog thing.

"You two are presidents of the Student Awareness Committee. You should be contributing," Angeline **hissed**, but she didn't really hiss exactly. It was more like **"pleasantly chirped."** But I'm pretty sure that a hiss was implied.

Isabella said that the blog sounded too much like homework and she already has a ton of homework from math and science and social studies to ignore, so she doesn't think she can find the time to ignore more.

Then Angeline pointed out that the whole school reads this blog, and it would be great for them to have the benefit of my observations.

I can only blow off so much per day.

Look, Blondy, I know when I'm being manipulated. I have dogs that are always begging for food, I have a best friend who is always trying to get me to do something hazardous, and most of all, I have **PARENTS**, okay, and they try it **ALL** the time.

So don't try to flatter me in order to get me to contribute.

I'm a ROCK, Angeline.

I'm not going to BUDGE.

You can't tell but I am really attractive for a rock

This little attempt of Angeline's is exactly the type of thing that people say in order to trick you into doing something. They think you are so conceited that you will actually believe everyone is just dying to have you do this thing or that thing.

Seriously, who would **really** believe that the whole school would benefit from their blog entries?

Unless it's **absolutely true**, of course, like it is in my case.

Angeline, you don't need to bother using pretend flattery when **real** flattery is completely accurate.

Oh, Miss Rose. Your head is TOTALLY PRETTY And smells better than all other heads.

Yeah. I got it, Blond Spider.

I know.

Dear Dumb Diary,

It happened.
It was exactly as I had feared.
Mom left a shirt on my bed this morning that she made for me.
It was full of her love and hard work and deep commitment and, from the looks of it, probably a lot of **monkey vomit.**
Not real monkey vomit. Just the same colors, texture, and smeariness.

How they make the fabric

It was so ugly that at first I thought one of my dogs had eaten the other, and then became tremendously sick on my comforter.

No such luck.

I tried it on, because I figured that was the least I could do.

I'm pretty sure that, just for a moment, I noticed my reflection **making fun of me**. If this was my reflection's reaction — and, Dumb Diary, my reflection and I have been through **A LOT** together — it was hard to imagine just what sort of abuse I would endure if I wore the shirt to school.

I know my mom didn't have to worry about this sort of thing when she was growing up, what with all the kids wearing the same **period costume**, but it's different today, Mom. We have **fashion** now, and we all have sophisticated electronic devices to help us make fun of the people who do fashion wrong.

I have never known anybody as mean as my reflection.

But she **IS** my mom, and I do love her, and sometimes love means that you have to do things you don't want to do.

Like **lying** to the people you love.

So I decided to put the monkeyvomit shirt on over a regular shirt. Then I could just take it off at school before my friends saw it and **destroyed me forever**.

Mom was so happy to see me wearing it that I could hardly understand why people think dishonesty is a bad thing.

Dad drove me to school, and when we were halfway there I noticed his tie. It was monkeyvomit patterned. It matched my shirt.

"I bet you have a different tie in your briefcase," I said.

"I bet you're wearing a different shirt underneath that one," he said.

We looked at each other for a moment and then **sat in silence** for several blocks.

"It's best that we don't know the results of these bets," I said, unbuttoning monkeyvomit.

"I have no idea what we were just talking about," he said, loosening his tie.

Last time I saw a face like that, Stinker was trying to get out of his leash

In the afternoon, Angeline ran up to my locker and rudely interrupted a conversation that Isabella and I could have been having. (Of course she didn't see the monkeyvomit shirt. I had that stashed in my backpack.)

"We **doubled** the hits on the site!" she squealed squealfully.

Isabella pulled out the new iPad that her mean older brothers recently gave her without their knowledge.

"Show us," she said.

Angeline opened up the Student Awareness Committee site. "**See?** Look at the numbers! We had **FOUR** people read the blog last night."

TRANSLATING ISABELLA

stealing — surprise giving

lying — truth decorating

punching — high-speed closed-fist tickling

Isabella and I started laughing. I could actually hear our laughter echoing off the **flawless porcelain perfection** of Angeline's sad face.

"That's just embarrassing," I said.

"You're making the Internet cry," Isabella added. "You're making my iPad feel bad about itself."

Angeline looked **hurt**, which I am sensitive and caring enough to know should bother me. But then an expression suddenly flashed across her face that reminded me of Isabella, and I **shuddered**.

"Well, it's not my name there at the top of the page."

She was right. Isabella and I **are** the presidents of the Student Awareness Committee. Right there at the top of the page, just below the ad for Lou's Car Wash and just above Angeline's latest article ("Lambs Are Really Cute When They Do Cute Lamby Things"), we saw our names, **big and bold**, like the entire stupid site had been **our** stupid idea or something.

Instinctively, I tried to **rub our names off** with my fingers, but it's an iPad, so the names just got bigger, and I panicked for a second.

Nice work, Angeline.

iSad

You hurt an iPad's feelings

"We quit," Isabella said.

"Yeah. Take it down," I said.

"Let's see what Uncle Dan thinks about you two ignoring your responsibilities," Angeline said snottily, and started marching snottily toward the office.

You might remember, Dumb Diary, that Dan Devon is the assistant principal of our school. He's Angeline's uncle, and since he married my Aunt Carol last year he's my uncle now, too.

As she snottily stormed away, Angeline turned around just long enough to let us have a snotty glimpse of the puppy-dog eyes she was planning to snottily use on Assistant Principal Devon. They were so **big and watery and sad** that, for a moment, I was sure that there was a blinded puppy stumbling around someplace looking for the eyeballs that some snot had stolen.

"Hang on," Isabella said. She told me that Assistant Principal Devon just got over being angry about her selling some first graders earthworms by telling them that they were **baby boa constrictors**. She had to give the money back, wash some desks, and write a report about why it is wrong to paint stripes and eyes and fangs on a worm. Needless to say, Isabella doesn't feel like having any additional friction right now.

"People don't appreciate how hard it is to **customize a worm**," she said quietly.

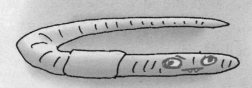
The Slippery-backed Squishy-viper

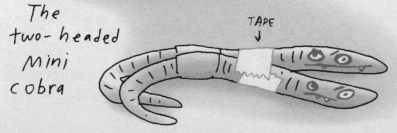
The micro-Rattler

The two-headed mini cobra

TAPE ↓

So we agreed to help Angeline with the stupid site we're presidents of. I told her maybe I'd try to come up with something to write about, just to protect our reputations. Isabella, who is so cute with how she's always **grubbing for money**, wanted to know about the car wash ad.

"That sponsor," Isabella said. "How did you get them to place an ad on your **derfy** little website?"

"He's a friend of my dad. We have a way to tell how many people click on his ad," Angeline explained. "The more people that click, the more Lou donates to the Student Awareness Committee. He only pays when people click."

Isabella began **clicking furiously** on the ad. She looked like a squirrel trying to crack open a nut with one finger. Squirrels might do that.

"Here comes my money," she said gleefully.

"It won't work," Angeline said. "The clicks have to come from different users. **The Internet is onto you,** Isabella."

Aww! Now I want a pet little squirrely who is greedy and dangerously unpredictable

As much as I would have loved to hang around and **be bored the rest of the way to death**, I had to go get my monkeyvomit shirt and cleverly put it back on in the girls' bathroom.

After I changed, I kept the shirt concealed under my jacket and ran out to the car, where Mom was waiting to pick me up. **Perfect timing.**

I must get my trickiness from Dad. When he came home from work tonight, he was confidently wearing his monkeyvomit tie. The three of us sat down to eat, and for the first time in a long time, Mom's dinner was not the **ugliest-looking** thing at the table.

Maybe Mom should use this fabric to make a tablecloth. Then everything she served would look **great** in comparison.

HEY! This could even help our Lunchroom Monitor and TALKING OX, miss Bruntford!

Compared to your dress, your face is only somewhat horrible

Best compliment she ever heard

THURSDAY 05

Dear Dumb Diary,

    Thursday used to be Meat Loaf Day. We would spend the first half of the day **fearing** lunch and the second half **regretting** it.

    We helped convince the school to stop having Meat Loaf Thursday, and they replaced it with **SURPRISE** Thursday. Now Bruntford (our lunchroom monitor) walks around taking little surveys where she asks you how much you either

  A.) Hate
    or
  B.) Especially hate

the new Thursday Special.

So. Do you like it?

Isabella and I were forming our opinion of today's Thursday Special, the **HOTDOG FIESTA** (which was nothing more than a sad little hotdog wobbling around in a taco shell), when Angeline flitted over and landed at our table like an enormous butterfly, only much flittier.

"Got something to write about?" she asked. "For our site?"

"I can't think of anything to write about," I said. "What are you writing about next?"

"This new menu item," she said, pointing one of her lustrously painted fingernails at my lunch. "I'm writing about the Hotdog Fiesta and how good it is."

"Good? **Are you joking?**" I asked. "'Fiesta' means 'party' in Spanish. This is more like a . . ." I turned to Isabella. "How do you say 'funeral' in Spanish?"

"*El funeral,*" she said. "Or *entierro.*"

"Isabella speaks Spanish?" Angeline asked, surprised.

I shook my head. "No. She just knows how to say 'funeral' in a lot of different languages."

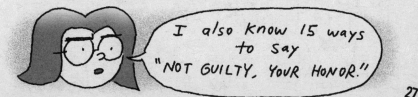

I also know 15 ways to say "NOT GUILTY, YOUR HONOR."

FRIDAY 06

Dear Dumb Diary,

Today, Isabella showed me our Student Awareness Committee site again. 53 people liked Angeline's story about the Hotdog Fiesta. That's a **record number** of likes. There's a little section under the article where people can leave their comments, and that's where things get really weird.

"Awesome story," one person wrote.

"I guess those hotdog things are pretty good," a different **dope** said.

"I hated them until I read your article. Now I love them," said another **misguided halfwit.**

Isabella tapped the screen on her ~~brothers'~~ iPad.

"And look — she says that tomorrow she's writing something about how much she likes to run laps in gym."

Isabella pointed out that Angeline might be influencing public opinion. Soon, **everybody** will see **everything** the way Angeline does. Isabella said that even though Angeline isn't as bad as many of the diseases we've read about, **one** Angeline seems to be about as many as the world should have to deal with, in spite of the fact that it seems to be able to deal with **many** diseases.

I told her that I didn't think Angeline's dumb little blog posts meant anything to anybody.

"You remember how long it took you to finally get rid of the meat loaf? How many of those Hotdog Fiestas are you prepared to eat?" Isabella asked dramatically. "And don't forget the **other things** they've tried to substitute for meat loaf."

Isabella is sleeping over tonight. Right after dinner, my mom gave her a great big surprise. A **REALLY BIG SURPRISE.**

My mom made Isabella **a skirt and hat.**

Isabella kicks people far more than the average person kicks people, and when you do that in a skirt, there's a **huge issue** of not broadcasting your underwear for the whole world to see because:

A.) It's embarrassing.

and

B.) All the people who saw the underwear have to be kicked as well, and the whole process begins all over again.

and

C.) Who has time for that?

So Isabella **hates** skirts. But even though she hates them, and even though this particular skirt was ugly even compared to my monkeyvomit shirt, Isabella accepted it, said thank you, and ran off to the bathroom and put it on. She even wore the matching hat.

We were all watching that reality show on TV with those awful people that say awful things to one another, and when my mom got up to leave the room, I asked Isabella if she really liked the skirt.

"Oh, heck no," she said right away, and my dad laughed quietly.

"Then why were you in such a hurry to put it on?" I whispered.

"Jamie, my grandma is always making me horrible clothes. I know all about these things. The sooner you wear them, the sooner you spill something on them or tear out a seam. With stuff this ugly, you must **never** delay, Jamie. You have to **wear it fast and wear it hard.**"

Dad and I looked at her in awe. How can she scheme so well?

Probably like how spiders poop what is basically LACE

Dad jumped up and ran out of the room. Two minutes later he was in the kitchen, wearing his monkeyvomit tie.

"Who wants hot fudge sundaes?" he shouted merrily, waving the chocolate syrup bottle **recklessly**.

Unfortunately, not a drop got on the tie.

SATURDAY 07

Dear Dumb Diary,

Isabella and I had one of those days where you spend four hours trying to come up with something to do, and then, by the time you come up with something, there's no time to do it, so you just watch TV in positions that make it look like maybe you were **born without bones**.

We do this about twelve times a month.

"Since we're not really doing anything, we should practice debate," I said.

"No, we shouldn't," Isabella said.

"We just did," I said.

Then Isabella hit me for tricking her into practicing debate.

ON saturdays we transform into bags of skin

"Maybe what we should do is have you write something for that dumb website," she suggested.

"That's not **US** doing something. That's **ME** doing something."

"Look," Isabella said. "We could spend hours going back and forth about why I see something one way and you see it the other, **wrong** way. The bottom line is that Angeline is currently writing circles around you, and I guess that means she's the better writer."

"HA," I said, really big like that. "I'm a better writer than she is and you know it." (Look how big I wrote that **HA**.)

Take THAT, Isabella

"Oh, I know, Jamie. It's just that, right now, **nobody else does**. The whole school is reading Angeline's entries and not yours."

She was right, but it made me so mad that I intentionally spilled soda on her pants so she would have to walk home wearing the **monkeyvomit** skirt.

(And hat, you know, because it really set off the ensemble.)

Other Outfits I would have liked for Her.

CACTUS COMBO

DIRTY BUCKET
AND
DIRTIER BUCKET

SLABS OF WET MEAT

SUNDAY 08

Dear Dumb Diary,

I started to read Angeline's entries on the Student Awareness Committee blog today. Here's one of them:

I like warm days. I don't like when it's very hot, and I don't like when it's very cold. Sometimes when it's only a little bit hot I don't mind it much. And sometimes when it's only a little bit cold I don't mind it much. In conclusion, I like warm days.

— Angeline

P.S. And kind-of-warm days.

It was a great entry because I've always wondered what sort of thing we'd get to read if a blog post was written by **a fart**. Like, a real fart. Like if a **mindless odor-cloud**, with no personality or purpose, stopped drifting around a room for a moment, somehow learned how to press the keys on a keyboard, and wrote a few lines about the weather before it just dissolved into thin air and was blamed on the dog. I had always wondered that.

And then I read the responses to her post, which got **67 likes**, now the current record.

"Oh, Angeline, you really nailed it. LOL! Warm days! LOL!"

"I liked the part about the warm days. Wow!"

"I agree about the cold days and also about the days that aren't very cold."

Angeline is slowly turning **everybody** into farts.

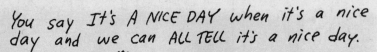

WARNING SIGNS YOU MAY BE A FART

You say It's A NICE DAY when it's a nice day and we can ALL TELL it's a nice day.

Everything is just the best thing ever ever ever ever EVER ever ever ever EVER EVER EVER

You are made of a horrible-smelling cloud or you are a very pretty blond. Especially the blond part.

MONDAY 09

Dear Dumb Diary,

It's clear that Mr. Smith's wig was designed for men with thinning hair who want to create the illusion that they are balancing a Yorkshire terrier on their heads. This is not really appealing to anybody, except maybe a **real** Yorkshire terrier during a flood.

In social studies today, he had us pair up with our partners for quiet practice debates. He gave us each a short list of subjects and said to just spend a couple of minutes on each one. He explained that one of us had to be **against** the things, and one of us had to be **for** them.

"I'll be for the things," Angeline said.

"But you haven't even read the list," I said.

"That's okay." She smiled. "I know that I'm for them."

Do you know how NICE you have to be to like things without knowing what they are? ♡

or how hard something really big had to kick your head?

How can somebody know that they're for something without even knowing **what it is**? I started just making up debate topics to test this theory.

"All right, Angeline," I said, pretending to read from the list. "Why are you for rainy days?"

"It's good for the plants, and you can stay inside and read a book."

Okay. Okay, maybe I could see that.

"How about the flu?" I said. "Why are you in favor of the flu?"

"Well, it helps you to appreciate the people that take care of you, and you feel so great when it's over."

I almost bit through my pencil.

"Okay, Blondy. How about getting struck by lightning?"

Angeline rolled her big fat eyes and batted her big fat eyelashes. **I'd done it.** Even Angeline couldn't come up with something good about getting struck by lightni —

"Well, it's a very rare occurrence. So, I guess it would make you famous," she said, SMILING.

SMILING.

SMILING about electricity shooting down from the sky and frying you on the sidewalk like an unsuspecting strip of bacon.

I wanted Mr. Smith to hear this, but just then, Miss Anderson — my art teacher, who is beautiful enough to be a **lady wrestler** but settled for being a teacher instead — walked by and waved. This caused Mr. Smith to adjust his wig, tell us to keep working, and trot out the door, calling to her about **some nonsense** he was clearly making up as an excuse to talk to her.

Teachers are attracted to other teachers. It's only natural. They date for a while, get married, buy a house, and start having little substitute teachers of their own.

FIND SOFTEST DIAPER
PRACTKE PEEK·A·BOO
SHAKE KEYS AT TEACHER
BLOW FARTS ON MY TUMMY

Baby Teachers drink coffee and assign homework almost from birth.

After Mr. Smith left, I tried a few more things on Angeline.

YOUR EYES FALL OUT.

I'll never ♥ need glasses. ♥

ALL THE HUMANS TURN INTO VAMPIRES.

Everybody looks great in black.

WOLVES EAT YOUR FAMILY.

Happy, well-fed wolves.

"Angeline! Are you some kind of mental case? Not everything has a **bright side**," I said, probably a bit too loud.

"Not everything has a **dark side**," she retorted.

"Try me," I said.

"Babies," she said smugly.

"Are you kidding? DIAPERS, Angeline. Give me a hard one."

"Sunny days," she said.

"**Sunburn.** C'mon, Angeline. Are you even trying?"

"Friendship," she said.

"**Don't answer that,**" Isabella interrupted.

I realized that Isabella had been listening to us, and listening closely. Fights never get past Isabella. She's always ready to either join in, or watch for loose change that falls out of pockets if people start to wrestle.

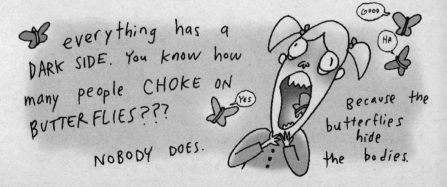

everything has a DARK SIDE. You know how many people CHOKE ON BUTTERFLIES???

NOBODY DOES.

GOOD

HA

YES

BECAUSE the butterflies hide the bodies.

"Why don't you two piranhas settle this like adults?" she said softly.

"What are you suggesting?" Angeline asked.

"Well, Angeline seems to like everything. Jamie seems to dislike everything. **Only one of you can be right,**" Isabella said, and for some weird reason, I felt like Isabella was setting some sort of giant mousetrap and was slowly edging us toward the cheese.

"Nobody likes mean, negative people, Jamie," Angeline said. "Why do you think everything is so terrible?"

"It's better than stumbling around like a fool, saying that everything is so great all the time," I said. "Nobody respects people who are cheerful all the time. They think they're dumb."

"You couldn't go **a month** without saying something mean," Angeline said.

"Yeah, well, you couldn't go **a month** without saying something nice," I blasted back.

Hey Angeline, I'm positive, too.

I'm positive you're dumb.

"**You wanna bet?**" she asked.

"You got it," I said. I'm pretty sure betting is against some kind of school rule, but Mr. Smith was still out of the room.

"Okay," she said. "The loser has to —"
Isabella interrupted.

"The loser has to play **Dare or Worse Dare** with me," she said quietly.

I lunged to cover Angeline's mouth. I had to stop her from agreeing. Angeline had no idea what Isabella was talking about.

Isabella stopped playing regular old Truth or Dare back in first grade. The problem with regular Truth or Dare is that the Truth part never really works. Somebody chooses Truth knowing that they can just lie, and then the asker has been swindled.

And Isabella can't deal with being swindled.

So Isabella invented **Dare or Worse Dare**.

The problem with Dare or Worse Dare is that **nobody, anywhere, ever,** should play it with Isabella.

This is not just my opinion. This is an ordinance in several counties.

You see, Isabella **customizes** her dares. She crafts each one especially for the person being dared. These are handmade dares, assembled one at a time, based on the specific weaknesses of the player.

The last time I played her was in third grade. She dared me to sneak into the cemetery with her and lie down for thirty minutes, with my eyes closed, on the grave of Abner Hogsnetter.

Spooky people

Love Spooky Lighting

When he was alive, Abner had been a clown. An old, cranky clown. He called himself **"Hoggy."** I knew him as "Hoggy with the doggy."

The first time I ever met Abner was at Shannon Nichol's birthday party, way back in first grade. Abner was the entertainment, and he was twisting balloon animals for all the kids.

I didn't want to go **anywhere near him**, but they made everyone get a balloon animal.

"What's your name?" he asked in between coughs.

"Jamie," I said, looking at his dirty clown costume.

"That's a nice name. What kind of animal do you want, Jenny?"

"I don't want one," I said, eyeing the clown makeup that was beginning to flake off the wrinkly parts of his face.

"Okay, a nice doggy," he said, blowing up the balloon and twisting it into shape.

I took it and **ran away** as fast as I could.

But I tripped and fell directly on top of my balloon dog.

And it popped.

I suppose that a great deal has already been written about what the inside of a clown's lungs smells like, but until you've really been smothered in it, wallowed in it, and inhaled it yourself, it's really **quite hard** to describe.

It's like a combination of wet raw chicken, cigar smoke, cotton candy, and socks. With hints of makeup and a kind of sad bitterness.

The experience was made worse by everybody's insistence that Hoggy make me a replacement balloon dog right away, which I carried around for the remainder of the party like a **grenade** that could go off at any second.

When we got home, I made Dad bury it.

I think it might have been a little bit alive

After that, we crossed paths several more times — at parties, or if a store had a big sale and they'd hired Hoggy to stand out front and attract customers. That clown worked for cheap, I guess, so he was always the one you'd see.

Hoggy remembered me as that little girl (Jenny, Janey, and one time, **Fred**) who was so upset when her balloon dog popped.

"How about a new doggy?" he'd call to me every time, as I **hid** behind somebody. Eventually, when I got invited to birthday parties, my parents had to ask ahead of time if Hoggy was going to be there.

The truth is, Hoggy is the reason I'm so **creeped out** by clowns.

Who laughs ALL THE TIME? psychopaths. That's who.

ALL that MAKE-UP? I'm sure it's to hide their identities.

GLOVES? To CONCEAL fingerprints I bet.

SILLY BOW TIES? Okay I kind of like the BOWTIES

So after Isabella dared me to lie down on his grave, I asked her what the **Worse Dare** was. She wouldn't tell me, but she said it involved a shovel.

I didn't demand details.

And so I lay there. **Trembling.** Every seven or eight minutes, Isabella would scream something like, "It's him! It's Hoggy the clown! Run, Jamie!"

If I opened my eyes or got up, I would have to start my thirty-minute dare all over again.

I had to restart so many times that eventually Isabella didn't find it funny anymore and we went home, where I took an hour-long shower to wash off the clowngrave dirt.

ABNER HOGSNETTER CREEPY DEAD CLOWN

And now back to Angeline's dumbness —

"Deal," Angeline said boldly.

I couldn't very well let Angeline be braver than me.

"Deal," I said quietly. I sensed that deep in the earth, a pair of decaying, bony fingers was slowly pulling a rotting balloon out of a baggy, checkered pants pocket.

"How about a **new doggy**, Jeanie?" Hoggy cackled.

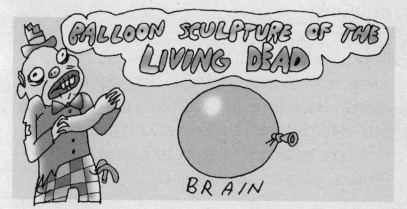

BALLOON SCULPTURE OF THE LIVING DEAD

BRAIN

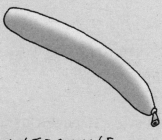

INTESTINE

SOME GROSS DEFLATED ORGAN OR SOMETHING I DON'T KNOW I HATE CLOWNS

TUESDAY 10

Dear Dumb Diary,

I didn't see any reason to waste time. There was no way that I was going to lie down on Abner Hogsnetter's grave again. So before school, I posted something on our blog to end this thing before it even begins. My post was **brief** and **brilliant**:

I'd just like to congratulate Hudson Rivers and his soccer team on a fine victory in last week's game against Wodehouse Middle School. I think everybody here at the Student Awareness Committee is a big fan of soccer, although I'm not sure about Angeline. Angeline, what do you think of soccer?

— Jamie

Pretty clever, huh? Let's see you **not** say something nice about this, Ang.

I didn't have to wait long.

She struck back in Mrs. Curie's science class this morning.

I'm pretty sure Mrs. Curie has a crush on diseases. All teachers are probably fascinated with them. A disease is like a test that nature gives your body. You want to get an A, but you'll be happy if you **just don't fail**.

Today she wanted to talk about gum disease, which is the most common complaint on Earth, unless you count the complaints of kids having to learn about it.

One of the main contributing factors is not brushing and flossing regularly. You need to brush your teeth at least twice a day and pretend to floss every day, but at the very least do it before you go to the dentist, because it's super embarrassing when you tell him you floss all the time and he pulls a little chunk of coconut out from between your teeth.

"Hey, where did **THAT** come from? I haven't had coconut in weeks!" you'll say, immediately realizing what an idiot ~~I sounded like~~ you sound like.

Don't bother lying to dentists

Mrs. Curie was showing gruesome pictures of gum disease up on her big monitor. When one came up that was particularly nasty, Angeline **pounced**.

"Hey, Jamie, what do you think of that guy?" she asked, loud enough for everyone to hear.

Isabella folded her arms and waited for my answer. A small smile curled on her lips. She clearly thought I'd have to say something mean. But I wasn't ready to lose this bet.

"I think that guy is, uh, pretty brave to be photographed like that, just to teach people about gum disease," I said, and the other kids in the class nodded in agreement.

Isabella angrily slouched in her chair and Angeline gave me her **ugliest scowl**, which — just being honest here — is still a **fairly attractive scowl**.

You aren't the only one who can fake this positive garbage, Angeline.

Normal Human Scowl

Abnormal Angeline Scowl

WEDNESDAY 11

Dear Dumb Diary,

Dad burst into my room this morning before my alarm clock went off.

(Alarm clocks have horrible lives. They do one of the most important jobs in the house, and everybody hates them for it.)

"Don't ask questions," he said, pushing a shopping bag toward me. **"Don't ask questions."**

"What are you doing?" I asked, totally not following instructions.

"Jamie? Are you up yet?" my mom said from the hallway.

Dad tore open the bag and, in a panic, pushed a shirt into my hands.

"Say, 'Oh my gosh, thanks, Dad,'" he whispered urgently. "You say that. **Say it now.**"

"Oh. My. Gosh. Thanks. Dad," I said flatly, just as Mom walked in, holding an animal that she had recently run over with her car, and then backed over for good measure, and then sewed buttons on.

Except that it wasn't an animal. It was **another shirt** she had made for me.

"Oh, wow!" Dad said with this kind of fakey enthusiasm. "Two shirts! Two new shirts for Jamie. Look, honey, I got her one, too. Such an odd coincidence. Well, I guess she should wear the one I got her first since I gave it to her first well good-bye you two have a nice day! **I was first.**"

Dad was down the stairs and out the front door in three steps.

our living room is never really this tidy

Mom looked confused and then shrugged.

"I made you another shirt, Jamie," she said. "But it looks like Dad already . . ."

"Yeah," I said. "This is kind of a new thing for Dad, huh?"

I said that since this **IS** kind of a brave new attempt for Dad, buying me clothes and all, that we shouldn't discourage him. And even though I really loved the new monkeyvomit shirt she made me, we should probably not hurt Dad's feelings.

Mom nodded in agreement, and I dodged the monkeyvomit for another day.

I **totally** owe Dad a favor.

GREAT WAYS TO PAY BACK DADS

promise to NEVER TURN INTO A WOMAN.

promise to never break, scratch, stain, or crack anything in the house again.

seriously, My dad would rather I turned into a bat.

And when I got to school, I learned why I owed him a **BIG** favor: Today was **picture day**. I wonder if Dad knew and wanted to save me from being photographed in monkeyvomit.

The Classic Picture Day Fails

Weird eye thing. Nobody but your Grandma will want one.

Photographer makes you pose in some peculiar position. Grandma will still take one.

Expression you have never made before. Grandma still wants one even though she's not sure who it is.

THURSDAY 12

Dear Dumb Diary,

Dad **DID** know. After dinner last night, I was doing homework at the kitchen table and he leaned in and quietly proved it.

"How do you think that shirt I gave you is going to look in your picture?"

I told him how glad I was, and that I owed him one.

"ONE?" He laughed. "You owe me a lot more than one for that, kid. Can you imagine having to look at that photo the rest of our lives?"

After dinner, I checked the Student Awareness Committee blog. Angeline had posted her response to my soccer post. Remember, I wrote:

I'd just like to congratulate Hudson Rivers and his soccer team on a fine victory in last week's game against Wodehouse Middle School. I think everybody here at the Student Awareness Committee is a big fan of soccer, although I'm not sure about Angeline. Angeline, what do you think of soccer?

— Jamie

And she responded:

Those little turds at Wodehouse Middle School got the beating they deserved.

— Angeline

Holy smokes, Angeline, how brutal can you get? A **BEATING**? Nice sportsmanship.

And everybody always thought you were so sweet. I can't wait to see how revolted they all are by their precious little Angeline now that they see she's in favor of **BEATINGS**.

Does she have other Dark Secrets?

Only uses nice handwriting to make others' look BAD

Only keeps lips moisturized so horrible words slide out easier

Grows eyelashes like that in the hopes somebody will get tangled in one and fall

FRIDAY 13

Dear Dumb Diary,

The soccer team was so revolted with Angeline's bad sportsmanship that, out of pure disgust, they got to school early and decorated her locker with ribbons and balloons.

They put a sign saying **ANGELINE: NUMBER ONE FAN** in big cutout letters on her locker door, and used gold and silver glitter to signify how **disappointed** they were in her post.

I'm sure the letter jacket they gave her was also supposed to let her know just how **deeply sickened** they were by her post.

As I stood there, staring, Isabella slid up beside me silently, in the way only an anaconda or Isabella can do.

"What do you think of all this?" she asked me.

I snorted. "I hope Angeline takes that jacket, and . . ."

I knew that if I said something unpleasant, I'd lose the bet.

". . . I hope she takes that jacket and wears it with pride. It's really nice of them to honor her that way," I finished.

Isabella made that sound that spiders make when a fly avoids their web instead of plowing right into it.

I don't know what that sound is. **Somebody knows.** Spider scientists know.

"It's weird, isn't it?" Isabella said. "Angeline says something mean and people love her for it. It's like she's **stealing your essence.**"

Just then, Hudson walked over.

"Thanks for the post on your blog," he said to me. "You should come watch us play sometime."

He walked away with a smile, and Isabella and I looked at each other.

I immediately wondered if maybe, just maybe, there could be something **good** about goodness that the human mind can't comprehend.

WAIT COULD THAT MEAN BADNESS MIGHT SOMEHOW BE SLIGHTLY BAD?

Strictly speaking, many of my posts to the Student Awareness Committee blog probably have very little to do with Student Awareness, but let's face it, as far as students go, I can come up with LOTS more interesting things to be aware of.

As an experiment, I put a new post up on our blog. First, I need to make it clear, Dumb Diary, that I **HATE** mushrooms. If planet Earth had a nose, I'm sure that mushrooms are what it would pick out of that nose, if Earth also had a finger.

But I couldn't say that. So here's what I said:

Mushrooms on a pizza? My mom loves 'em. But make mine pepperoni.

— Jamie

See? I didn't come right out and say that mushrooms are squeaky little wads of soil and snot. I said something nice about them — I said that **somebody else** loved them.

The edible ones are no more appealing than the poisonous ones

I waited, and within a few minutes, a few people said that they also loved pepperoni, and green peppers, and bacon.

Soon, the post was up to 72 likes — a new record. It turns out that there are a lot of people in the world who respond well to niceness.

Weirdos.

SATURDAY 14

Dear Dumb Diary,

No school today. No plans. But as I was staring into space, Isabella's wisdom on homemade clothes came back to me. There was only **one thing** to do.

"Hey, Mom. Can I have that new shirt you made me now?"

She was so happy I asked for it that she didn't even question the fact that I wanted it on a Saturday.

To work in the yard.

Cleaning up my beagles' turds.

And you just GOTTA be styling when you do poop things.

But when I got outside, Dad was already busy cleaning up.

In his tie.

And he was purposely leaning **waaaay** over so that the tie would dangle enticingly in front of Stinkette's nose. Stinkette is still a puppy, and will chew on just about anything.

But not Dad's monkeyvomit tie.

He didn't know I had come outside, and I startled him as he was trying to push the tie into Stinkette's mouth.

"I WAS NOT DOING ANYTHING TO IT JUST NOW IN THE DOG'S MOUTH," he blurted out before he realized that I wasn't Mom.

"Don't sneak up on me, Jamie," he said, exhaling hard. "Now, tell your dog to eat my tie."

"**Eat his tie**, Stinkette," I ordered.

Stinkette stared stupidly, one eye wandering slightly.

"It won't work, Dad," I said. "These beagles only want to eat the things you don't want them to eat. Trust me. I've put beef gravy on homework. They can sense what you want, and they live to deny you these things."

"What are we supposed to do?" he whined pathetically.

"I dunno, Dad."

He held up the bag of turds he had scooped and smiled hopefully.

"Do you think Mom would believe it if we said we got in a **turd fight** wearing her handmade clothes?"

For a moment I actually thought I might want to get hit with a flying Dog turd.

Don't worry. We didn't have a turd fight. But I liked the way Dad was thinking, and it inspired me to spill on my shirt at dinner. His eyes lit up, and then he intentionally spilled on his tie when Mom was out of the room.

"Oh, nuts!" she said, sitting back down at the table. "Look at you two."

We made our best **WE ARE ASHAMED OF OURSELVES** faces.

"Good thing that fabric won't stain," she said. "Nope. That will all come off in the wash."

We made our best **WE ARE GRATEFUL THAT WE GET TO KEEP THIS WONDERFUL CLOTHING** faces.

I wonder how many times you can lie with your face before you just wear it out and it won't lie for you anymore.

I should probably stop facelying before I get OLD.

SUNDAY 15

Dear Dumb Diary,

Aunt Carol and Uncle Dan came over for coffee and donuts this morning. We don't really observe a lot of nutritional rules on Sunday mornings, because evidently, calories eaten on Sundays **don't count**.

You can have a frosted donut, or a frosted jelly-filled donut, or a frosted jelly-filled ox. Have **anything you want** to eat for Sunday breakfast.

Aunt Carol was bragging that Uncle Dan is getting some kind of educational award for his work as assistant principal at our school. I guess it's kind of a big deal. They're taking a picture of him and it's getting framed and hung in the hallway **until the end of time**, so that future civilizations can dig up our school and see how strange we looked with our normal-sized heads and clothing not made out of aluminum foil and bodies not fighting aliens, which is how movies tell us we will be spending most of our time in the future.

We all congratulated Uncle Dan through mouthfuls of breakfast. I think that if you're going to talk with your mouth full, it should be full of donuts. This way, the things you say will sound nicer, as they are covered with **deliciousness molecules.**

MONDAY 16

Dear Dumb Diary,

    More debate practice in social studies today. Everybody was paired off, so Isabella was working with Dicky Flartsnutt, and Angeline and I were having our small, private debates.

    "Pretty clever post about the soccer team," I said, carefully phrasing it in such a way as to be perfectly **nice**. I nodded toward the letter jacket draped over the back of her chair.

    "You wish that you had thought of it," Angeline said back, carefully selecting her words to be **mean**.

    "I'm learning how to pretend to be nice, like you," I said. "People like it. Did you see how many people liked my little mushroom post? Like seven people commented."

    "I'm learning, too," she said. "And I might never change back, you butt." There was something about the way she said "butt" — not the funny, joyous way that people usually say it — but something a bit sinister, like an **evil wizard** might say it.

    "Read my post tonight," she said.

And I did.

Angeline responded to my post about mushrooms. She wrote:

Jamie, who are you kidding about mushrooms?

They're a fungus. Know what else is a fungus? The stuff that grows in the grout in the shower.

They're named "mush" as a warning for what they're going to do when you bite down on them, and "room" because that's what you're going to be running from after that first bite.

They live in the dark, like some sort of miserable deformed little trolls. If you ever see me eating one, it means that somebody has kidnapped every single kitten on Earth, and the kidnappers have told me that unless I eat a mushroom, terrible harm will come to the kittens. Not just most of the kittens. Every. Single. One. It would take every single one.

— Angeline

I noticed that a few people had liked her post.

75 people.

SEVENTY-FIVE.

I called Isabella.

"Did you see how many people liked Angeline's post on mushrooms?"

"Sure did," she said. "This new, mean Angeline is even more popular than nice Angeline. Maybe you should write a post and really give her a piece of your mind."

Nope. Nope nope nope. "I know you're just trying to get me to lose the bet, Isabella. To be honest, I have to admit that I thought her post was pretty funny."

"I don't doubt that," Isabella said. "You wrote it."

It suddenly came back to me. **I did write that.** A year ago. In an email to Angeline. I slumped down hard on my bed and then slumped right up again because I had slumped on Stinker's face. I moved down and reslumped.

The Slumper

The Beslumped

"She can't do that," I said.

"Why not?" Isabella asked with a laugh. "Because it's mean to copy off people? Angeline is supposed to be mean now, so I'm going to allow it. But is there anything you want to say about it?"

There was a lot I wanted to say. But I wasn't going to lose this bet.

"NO."

ISABELLA: Life Long master of MEANNESS

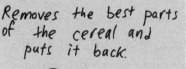

Removes the best parts of the cereal and puts it back.

Asks Santa for things an old fat man should not transport.

Knows your favorite parts of movies. Won't watch them on purpose.

Refused to cry when doctor slapped her in order to make the doctor question her own skills.

TUESDAY 17

Dear Dumb Diary,

I wasn't in a very good mood when I woke up today. I had dreamed that I was being chased by zombies but I wasn't allowed to hurt them, even in self-defense. I spent eight hours trying to **politely persuade** the zombies to spit out my arm. Exhausting.

I screamed a little when I woke up, because there was a grimy, hideous zombie torso dragging itself across my bed.

After a couple of blinks, I realized that Mom had slipped in while I was asleep and carefully laid a new homemade shirt across my bed. This one even had a little **happy face** embroidered on it.

Mom stuck her head around the corner and made me scream again.

"I was thinking that the little happy face could be, like, your thing. You know, because you're so happy all the time. I'll put it on everything. It will be your trademark!" she squealed.

I looked down at the happy face. He looked **happy-ish**, but not totally happy. He also looked a little mutated, and maybe a little too pleased about being mutated.

It would make somebody wonder if he was happy that the bear stopped mauling him halfway through the mauling, or maybe he was happy that the tree had fallen on only half his face, and not his whole face.

I smiled at Mom.

Ironically, I probably smiled the **exact same smile** that the embroidered happy-face guy was smiling.

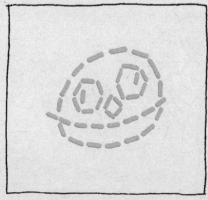

MUTATED SEWN GUY

MUTATED ME

"DAD, CAN YOU TAKE ME TO SCHOOL TODAY?" I shouted.

But there was no answer. A chill ran through me.

"Mom, where's Dad? I wanted him to drive me to school today."

She said he had left for work early. I looked down at my new monkeyvomit shirt. Embroidered guy smiled his mutated smile back up at me.

"You'll have to take the bus," Mom said.

That would mean wearing the shirt, and **everybody seeing**.

I thought back to happier times, when Mom and I would buy my clothes at a real store, made by real people with fabric that did not appear to have once lined a sick monkey's cage.

Mom would pick something up, and hold it up to my back to see if it fit. . . .

That was it.

Adorable
Lil'
← me

I sat on my bed and waited, calculating the timing so I'd be just a little late leaving the house. When the time was right, I ran out the front door, yelling good-bye to my mom.

I heard her yelling good-bye back to me as I left, and I knew she got a good look at her shirt as I ran away. She must have been so happy to see me wearing it.

Half of it, anyway.

I had remembered how Mom would hold up a shirt to my back to get an idea of how it would look. So all I had to do was tape the shirt to my back — and from behind, it would look like I was wearing it.

By the time I rounded the corner, the other kids were already piling on the bus, so they couldn't see anything but my front.

I made sure I was the last one on the bus. As I climbed on, I gave monkeyvomit one quick **tug** and wadded it up in my backpack.

NORMAL GIRL NOT WEARING MONKEY VOMIT

FREAK

79

I was so happy that I had fooled Mom **AND** made her happy in the process, that by the time we got to lunch, it wasn't even hard for me to make up something nice to say about the new menu item Bruntford was trying out.

It was her personal tribute to the Beatles — a giant plate of peas that she called **GIVE PEAS A CHANCE**. She held it out to me for an opinion.

"Gosh," I said sweetly. "Look at 'em all."

"Try it," Bruntford said.

"No, thanks."

"Have a taste," she insisted.

"No, thank you."

"Take a pea **right here, right now**," she said loudly, and everyone turned around to look. Bruntford suddenly understood how that sounded, and she just stood there, turning red, with her giant mouth gaping open.

Isabella leaned forward, eyes filled with hope, to hear my reaction.

OOPS

It was a **golden opportunity**, but I didn't say anything mean to Bruntford. I didn't even give her a dirty look. I just took a pea and smiled about how delicious it was.

I could see that Isabella was getting frustrated. She glared at Angeline. I think she is **finally** starting to sense that I'm not the one she should be working on.

After school, I ran home and hopped the fence into my backyard, which made both Stinker and Stinkette start barking at the back door, just as I had planned.

I waited a second, ran around to the front door, went inside, and sprinted up to my room, yelling, "MOM, I'M HOME!" Mom was, of course, letting the barking dogs out, so she didn't even see me. This gave me time to go in my room, change into the monkeyvomit shirt she thought I wore to school, and come back down.

It was almost **too easy**.

Adults— you should be MUCH HARDER TO FOOL.

After dinner, I checked our blog. It's getting more hits all the time. Isabella posted this tonight:

Isabella here. Haven't had a chance to run this by my partners at the Student Awareness Committee, so I'll just post it here for them to see. I think we need to really increase the amount of recycling we do at Mackerel, because a clean Earth is important to us all. Jamie and Angeline, what do you say?

— Isabella

I wasted no time in posting my response.

Awesome idea, Isabella. We should be working much harder on this. C'mon, who doesn't believe we need a cleaner planet?

— Jamie

Click click click. 85 likes.
And somewhere, tonight, if you close your eyes and listen carefully, you'll hear the sweet, soft sound of a blond head **exploding**.

WEDNESDAY 18

Dear Dumb Diary,

Today on the morning announcements they said something about Assistant Principal Devon getting this big award, and how his photo will go up in the hallway, and how he's a terrific example to us all, and Isabella stood up and started applauding.

It's weird, but applause is contagious, so everybody joined in. And then, as it started to die down, she looked at me and Angeline and I suddenly knew what her **devious plan** was.

"Angeline and Jamie, you guys must be extra proud, since Assistant Principal Devon is your uncle. This is pretty cool, huh?"

"**Awesome,**" I said, and glanced at Angeline, who was looking like she had perhaps just swallowed a **large burp** that belonged to somebody else.

One nice little word about Uncle Dan out of her nice little mouth and that would end it all. She would lose.

"I . . . uh . . ."

Angeline is super-proud of her uncle. She **couldn't possibly** say anything mean.

"I know I wouldn't want a big picture of me up in the hallway. It would be about five minutes before **you-know-who** drew a mustache on it," she said, and thumbed her little thumb at me.

People laughed, and Isabella's head hit the desk like a steel bowling ball hitting a sidewalk.

I hate to admit it, Dumb Diary, but Angeline is every bit as good at avoiding the traps as I am.

Nothing else sounds exactly like childhead

THONK

She proved it again later, in her response to Isabella's recycling question on the blog:

Isabella, I read your post about recycling. My opinion is that people who don't recycle are inconsiderate slobs.

— Angeline

And, of course, there were 90 likes and many joyful comments about her post.

She's good at being good, and she's good at being bad. Makes me wonder how she could be so ~~good at it all.~~ ~~Bad at it all.~~ Whatever.

Good people are good at being Bad....

They just do what they would never do.

THURSDAY 19

Dear Dumb Diary,

I had to go down to the school office today. I got gum in my hair and wanted Aunt Carol to get it out. Isabella offered, but I knew she would just pull it until I swore a lot and then I would have **lost the bet**. And I wasn't going down like that.

Aunt Carol is kind of an expert on **adult lady beauty**, anyway, so I'm sure she's read many fashion magazines featuring tips on gum removal.

FEMALE WOMAN MAGAZINE

IN THIS ISSUE

REMOVING GUM FROM HAIR GLAMOROUSLY

POSING IN THAT IDIOTIC WAY WHERE HOLD YOUR HEAD AND HIP WEIRDLY

FARTING CLEVERLY

She was so excited to see me, because she was in the middle of making Uncle Dan consider various coat, tie, and shirt combinations for his big award photo.

She was having a lot of fun, but he looked like a cat that knew it was getting a bath soon.

"Why couldn't we do this at home?" he asked. "We're missing lunch, and I'm **starving**."

"Because the light here is different than at home," she said with a smile. "The light affects how the photo looks. You always have to decide on these things using the same light you'll be photographed in."

Uncle Dan made a sound like his soul was escaping through his nostrils.

"This photo is going to hang in these halls until the end of time. Everybody will see it every day. It has to be **perfect**," she said.

Evidently he had a little bit of soul left in one nostril, and it escaped as well.

principals
possibly
have
souls
just like
people
Do

Aunt Carol held up tie after tie, tilting her head, as if seeing with a tilted head was better than seeing with a regular upright head.

She asked me what I thought.

I said that I thought I needed the gum out of my hair before I was late for class.

She opened her desk drawer and pulled out a huge jar of peanut butter.

"You have peanut butter here?" Uncle Dan said.

She smeared the peanut butter all over the gum, and it slid right out. Then she got out a jar of Vaseline and used that to get the peanut butter out of my hair. Then she used some adhesive-remover to get the Vaseline out of my hair.

"That's great stuff for getting out Vaseline," I said.

"Yeah," she said. **"It gets gum out, too."**

even though GLOP is gross, GLOP is the basis of all Beauty products

Yes. I know. But she was distracted with the important business of picking out her husband's clothes.

I closed the door behind me quietly, pausing for just long enough to glimpse Uncle Dan eating an enormous wad of peanut butter off a pen.

Pens can do so much for us.

FEELINGS HURTER

EMERGENCY MUSTACHE

FEELINGS FIXER

FRIDAY 20

Dear Dumb Diary,

Isabella and Angeline came by my locker this afternoon. Isabella said that she thought our blog needed a little **pizzazz**, which I was immediately in favor of, because at first I thought it had something to do with pizza.

It turns out that **pizzazz**, Dumb Diary, means eye-catching, or fun, or fancy.

Isabella thought maybe we should have a logo.

I told her I would get right on it, but she said she had it under control. "I know you have a lot to do what with all that stuff you have going on," she added.

Pizza!

Pizzazz!

PIZZA WITH PIZZAZZ!
(FAIRLY AWFUL)

"What stuff?" I asked. I didn't have any stuff going on except for cleaning my room, helping my dad get some junk out of the garage, a bunch of homework, and a stack of thank-you cards I still owed people from Christmas and my birthday, and another Christmas and another birthday.

"I've got this under control," Isabella said, smiling. Then she gave me a nice good-bye shove.

I'll get to them. I'll get to them.

Dear Uncle Joe,
Thank you for the nice rattle.
Love,
Jamie

When I got home, Dad had picked up Chinese food, which is how my dad often celebrates things.

He just found out that he's up for a promotion and raise at work, and he has a big review next week. He's only about halfway sure he's going to get it. His boss is a little stuffy, and he says he needs to be on his best behavior until then.

I made him a handy checklist of **how to be stuffy** until he gets the promotion.

Always extend pinky when licking butter knife.

Wear tuxedos at all times, including while showering.

Always wear a TOP HAT and MONOCLE to class things up when you cut your hideous DADFARTS.

SATURDAY 21

Dear Dumb Diary,

So today Dad lost the tie that my mom made him. He woke up early to get us donuts, and he decided to wear his tie to the donut shop. And when he was getting back into the car, he scratched himself **really, really, really, really** badly and had to keep himself from bleeding to death, so he used his tie to stop the bleeding.

And on the way home, he had his arm out the window and the tie blew off. He would have stopped, but it was right on that bridge down by Lincoln Road, so the tie fell in the river and it's long gone by now. Many people have reported seeing **bears** down near that spot, anyway.

And it's a good thing that Dad tried this **HUGE DUMB LIE** out on me first, because Mom would have seen right through it.

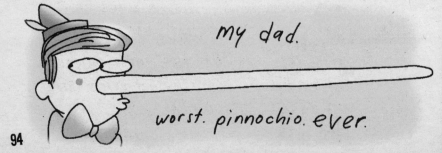

my dad.

worst. pinnochio. ever.

"Just for starters, Dad, you're wearing a T-shirt. Who wears a tie with a T-shirt? You go for donuts on Sunday, not Saturday, Lincoln Road isn't on the way, and you don't have a scratch on your arm. Not even a little one."

He shrugged and pulled his monkeyvomit tie out of his pocket.

"Did you believe the bear part?" he asked.

"No," I said. "Why can't you just keep taking the tie off on your way to work?"

"Because it's wrong to keep lying. It's deceitful and wrong, Jamie."

"You were just getting ready to tell a **huge lie** about bleeding to death," I pointed out.

He looked at me and knew I was right.

"You're grounded for that," he said. "You're grounded for suggesting that terrible plan. Sometimes your mom pops in unexpectedly for lunch, and your plan would get me busted. So I'm grounding you for giving me that **very terrible plan.**"

DUDE. I'm the ACTUAL BEAR and even I don't believe the BEAR PART.

"You're not grounding me," I said. "You're just frustrated. We'll figure this out, Dad."

He nodded. He knew he couldn't ground me. And besides, if you can't count on a middle school kid for a **reliable lie**, who can you count on?

Lies Invented by Middle Schoolers

1923

"My dog ate my homework."

9000 BC

"My Mastodon ate my homework."

100,000 BC

"ME EATED HOMEWORKS."

SUNDAY 22

Dear Dumb Diary,

Isabella called me and Angeline today about having an **emergency meeting** of the Student Awareness Committee at her house. She had never called for an emergency meeting before.

Isabella rarely uses the word **"emergency,"** so there were just a few questions I wanted to ask first.

1.) Is there an enormous fire that you need help putting out?
2.) Is there any kind of "thing" that you need help burying?
3.) Is there an enormous fire that you need help starting?

After she answered **"no"** to these three things, and I confirmed that there was nothing that would involve running from police or guard dogs, my mom drove me over to her house.

I might have preferred the guard dogs. Angeline was already there when I arrived. So was Dicky Flartsnutt, who was holding a poster board and dancing up and down, due to either excitement or a trip to the bathroom that was super incredibly **overdue**.

Isabella sat us down.

"I asked Dicky to design a logo," she began. "You know, for the Student Awareness Committee. I love it, of course, but I told him that we all had to **agree**."

I knew this wasn't going to go well.

"Dicky, could you please turn your drawing around? Let's get their opinions."

With a squeal of **delighted anticipation**, Dicky showed us his drawing.

Sweat Squirting excitement

paper crumpling excitement

Lip chapping excitement

Bowel tingling excitement Ew

"It's a clown," he said. "Isabella thought a clown would be a good idea, because they're so colorful and everybody likes them."

I wheezed.

Angeline squinted. "Hey, that looks a little like . . ."

"It is!" Isabella said with a grin. "It's our dear departed Hoggy the clown. Do you remember Hoggy, Jamie? He was a very popular local celebrity before he passed away. This will be a great **tribute** to him, don't you think?"

More wheezing.

"What do you think of Dicky's artwork?" Isabella asked Angeline. "He worked on it for hours, so be **honest**."

Isabella had thought this through. She knew that I couldn't deal nicely with a clown, and that Angeline wouldn't be able to hurt Dicky's feelings. **Somebody had to crack.**

"I love the idea of a logo," I said.

"Yes," Isabella said. "But **THIS** logo. What do you think of this **CLOWN** logo?"

"You shouldn't have made Dicky draw a clown," Angeline said. "You should have let him choose whatever he wanted. The logo doesn't even have to be a drawing."

Ah. **Very smooth**, Angeline. Nothing nice, but nothing directed at Dicky.

"Angeline's right," I said. "Dicky's creative, and he could easily come up with his own idea for the logo." Nice, right? Nothing mean there.

"FINE," Isabella said through her gnashing teeth. She turned to Dicky, her glasses gleaming. Mercifully, Dicky couldn't see the fire that burned inside her eyes behind the glare on the lenses.

"Dicky," she said, continuing to talk through her teeth, "what would you like to use for a logo?"

Dicky had no power to resist her.

"A clown," he said meekly.

Isabella smiled.

"You two warts happy now?" she asked us.
"Now what do you guys say to the clown?"

"**I'm not sure**," Angeline said.

I echoed her. "I'm not sure, either."

Not negative, not positive, not nice, not
mean. It was the perfect way to respond if you don't
care that it makes you sound **very, very dumb**.
I don't know why I never thought of it before. Since
Angeline is a blond, it's possible that she's just
more fluent in dumb.

Isabella started to muscle the three of us to
the door.

"Fine. A clown it is. Time to go home,
everybody. Meeting over."

she's not a fan
of long good-byes

Outside on the porch, as we all waited in the rain for our rides, I considered asking Angeline rapid-fire questions about what she thought of Dicky's rubber shoes, or his strange pants, or his shirt with a design that was clearly meant for a much younger wearer. But I had the feeling that she might be able to dodge **every question**.

I noticed that Dicky was holding his drawing behind his back, so he didn't realize that the paint was washing off the poster board and down Isabella's steps. I thought about how proud he was of the logo, and how hard he had worked on it, and how now it would never get used.

I nearly told him, but then I thought about how Isabella's mom would probably make her **clean it up**, so I didn't say anything.

Good-bye, Hoggy.

MONDAY 23

Dear Dumb Diary,

Today when I opened my locker, I found a little gift-wrapped box with a note on it that said:

Let's end this bet.
Signed, Angeline

It was in her pretty lacy handwriting, and it smelled of her delicious strawberry scent, which she secretes naturally the way normal people secrete sweat. I kind of knew she wouldn't be able to take the pressure, so I wasn't surprised at her little gift offering.

I opened it happily, and **100 spiders** crawled out.

You can't climb the air. I've seen others try, I tried it today, and it can't be done. As hard as you pretend that there's an invisible ladder for you to go up, it won't be there, and you'll end up just standing in place, flapping and screaming.

After I calmed down, I realized what Angeline's little note meant. She was planning on ending the bet when I went nuts on her for leaving me the spiders.

I picked up the empty box (spiders are, evidently, afraid of girl screams so they ran away), and marched down the hall with it toward Angeline's locker.

When I got there, she was smiling and holding a box almost identical to mine.

It had a little note on it that said:

It looked like my handwriting, and it even had glitter all over it, which is my thing. Totally my thing.

It was full of chocolates.

"Did you put this here for me?" she asked. "Because I was thinking that if you had, I should come and say **something nice**."

"No. Did you leave a box of spiders in my locker?" I said. "Because if you had, I probably would have said **something really mean**."

"One of us would have lost," Angeline said with a frown. "Isabella did this. What a dirty trick. I'm going to find her right now."

"I'll go with you," I said.

When we found Isabella, Angeline started to yell at her.

"This is low, even for you, Isabella. Of all the rotten ways to make us lose this bet . . ." She turned to me, giving me the chance to take a crack at her.

I opened my mouth to say something, but then I hesitated. Gift wrap and glitter costs money. Those chocolates were expensive, and not a single one was missing from the box.

"**Very clever,** Angeline," I said sweetly. "You almost had me. But Isabella would never spend the cash, and she would have never been able to part with the chocolate. **You** sent me the box, and you made one for yourself in order to frame Isabella."

"Well, aren't you a smart little goatface," Angeline said, dropping the box and walking away.

"Did she really come up with that?" Isabella asked through a mouthful of floor chocolate. "That's pretty **diabolical.**"

TUESDAY 24

Dear Dumb Diary,

Mrs. Curie is still all about the diseases. We talked about antibiotics in science today, and I remembered seeing something on a yogurt container saying it was full of probiotics.

"Mrs. Curie, are we antibiotic or probiotic?" I asked, feeling that maybe we were sending **mixed messages** to the biotics.

"Well, they're good sometimes and bad other times," she said. Then she went on to tell us about all different kinds of these little fellas, and how some help us, and some harm us.

I thought it was weird how they all have this **huge** effect on us, but none of them even have the brainpower to know that we exist. Doesn't it seem like we should be able to trick them into infecting mannequins? Or even photographs of ourselves?

REAL HUMAN FOR GERMS TO ATTACK

After class, I talked to Isabella about Angeline's little plot yesterday.

"I can hardly believe that Angeline did that," Isabella said. "Seriously, that is some **quality scheming**. I think I may have a position for her in my organization. She's a natural."

Is she? I mean, how could sweet little super-nice Angeline even operate on that level?

I'm not sure what ORGANIZATION ISABELLA is TALKING ABOUT

But I'm pretty sure it would be one of those that James Bond always has a problem with

WEDNESDAY 25

Dear Dumb Diary,

Before school today, Assistant Principal Devon stopped me in the hall and asked me to come to his office.

He pulled a little box from his desk drawer and showed it to me. It was a necklace — a beautiful little gold heart on a chain.

"What do you think?" he said.

"Thanks!" I said, reaching for the necklace, which he quickly pulled away.

"No, it's not for you. It's for your Aunt Carol. Thursday is our one-year anniversary."

"No, it isn't," I said.

"Yes, it is," he said.

"NO. IT. ISN'T."

"YES. IT. IS. It's the one-year anniversary of our engagement."

I had to count on my fingers. Oh, man. He was right.

Since Uncle Dan is one of the **Very Recently Married,** he actually remembers things like this. My dad doesn't remember any dates, not even his actual wedding anniversary, much less the dumb unofficial anniversaries like engagements. To prevent problems, my mom writes reminders and tapes them to his underwear.

One time, he missed one until he got to a doctor's appointment. He pulled off his pants and the doctor saw a note that read, *IT'S SOMEBODY'S BIRTHDAY* taped to my dad's underpants. The weird thing was, it really was his doctor's birthday.

Now he has a different doctor.

I asked Uncle Dan if Aunt Carol knew it was their engagement anniversary, and he laughed.

"Of course she knows, Jamie! Your Aunt Carol is **very sentimental** about things like this."

Aunt Carol stopped by the house kind of late tonight — she was dropping off a carton of milk that she had picked up for my mom at the store. I was already in my pajamas. And by pajamas, I mean clothes I probably should have thrown out but am still willing to wear under blankets in the dark.

My pajamas are all pretty much HOBO-READY.

"Shopping, huh?" I asked, grinning. I figured she had been out buying an anniversary gift for Uncle Dan.

"Yes," she said, looking puzzled.

"Getting something nice for Uncle Dan?"

"I got him some peanut butter for his lunches. I never knew how much he liked it before."

"You know what I mean," I said. "Your anniversary. It's tomorrow."

"No, it's not," she said, and we kind of recreated the entire conversation I'd had earlier with Uncle Dan.

Finally, after counting on her fingers, she admitted it.

"Oh, I guess it is," she said. "But I'm not going to worry about it. I'm sure he didn't remember."

Dad nodded. He agreed that nobody should remember anything.

I made a groany, burpy swallowing sound, and Mom and Aunt Carol eyed me suspiciously.

"He **DID** remember, didn't he?" Aunt Carol said. I tried to make it up the stairs without responding, but when anniversary presents are involved, old ladies like Mom and Aunt Carol can move a lot faster than you think, and they caught me before I was even halfway up.

"He did remember," I said, knowing that they could torture it out of me anyway. Why delay things? "He got you a beautiful necklace, and he's so excited to give it to you."

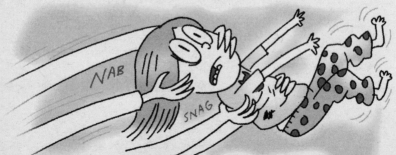

NOBODY CAN ESCAPE THE CLUTCHES OF TWO LADIES

Aunt Carol started freaking out. Most of the stores were closed, and there was really no time to go shopping anyway because she was already late. Then Uncle Dan would totally know she had waited until the **last second** to get him something.

I went into the kitchen and quickly put together a fine assortment of canned goods in a basket with a ribbon. I made a glittery little card that read:

I was pretty proud of the idea, but when I brought it back out into the living room, Aunt Carol had calmed down.

"It's a great idea, Jamie," she said in that voice adults use when something is **not** a great idea. "But we figured it out."

My dad smiled and nodded.

THURSDAY 26

Dear Dumb Diary,

Today was the day they took Uncle Dan's photo. Aunt Carol even got me and Angeline out of class so we could be part of his **big moment**.

The cameraman had set up some big fancy lights, and was fussing over every detail in the background.

Before they took the photos, Uncle Dan grabbed Aunt Carol around the waist and pulled her close. It was so manly that I wanted to scream.

"Happy anniversary," he said, handing her the little box. She opened the necklace, put it on right away, and looked like she might cry.

"I got something for you, too," she said, handing him a box.

He laughed and hugged her and opened it — it was full of **monkeyvomit**.

It was Dad's monkeyvomit tie.

"It's beautiful!" Uncle Dan said.

At first I thought he was just being polite, but then I realized that Uncle Dan is almost a teacher, and teachers really love **ugly ties** best of all.

"Did you make this?" he asked her, his eyes filled with admiration.

He pulled off his old tie and put on the new one. Aunt Carol shot me a look to indicate that I had better not say a word.

"I did," she lied.

Angeline nudged me.

"That tie," she whispered. "That horrible tie is going to be around his neck in that photo until **the end of time.**"

I responded carefully, so as not to lose the bet.

"I didn't realize that you knew so much about men's fashion, Angeline," I whispered back.

"He can't wear that," she whispered louder. "Do something."

"**You** do something," I whispered back.

"She's **YOUR** aunt."

"She's your aunt now, too," I said, but I knew Angeline was right.

Uncle Dan stepped in front of the camera, and the cameraman scowled a bit.

"Going with that tie, are you?" he asked.

"**I sure am,**" Uncle Dan said proudly. "My wife made it for me."

I realized that I had no choice. I was going to **lose** the bet.

"Uncle Dan, can I say something?"

"Sure, Jamie, what is it?"

I took a deep breath. "It's about that tie."

"Okay. What's on your mind?" he asked kindly.

"If we were to take three feet of wrappings off a decaying mummy, drag it through a pigsty, dip it in toad slobber, and leave it at the bottom of a birdcage for six years, we would have a tie that would still be **a thousand times better-looking** than that smeary mess you have tied around your neck right now."

I also may have said a swear word or two in there. I don't remember. It was three weeks' worth of mean coming out **all at once**.

Uncle Dan just stood there with his mouth open.

Aunt Carol did the same.

The cameraman nodded in agreement and chimed in.

"In particular, the kid's right about the **toad slobber**," he said.

Angeline picked up the other tie.

"This one, on the other hand, is beautiful. It's classy, and dignified, and exactly the look we want for our beloved uncle and respected assistant principal," she said, handing it to him as though it was some sort of priceless artifact.

Okay maybe

not this priceless

"**They're right,**" Aunt Carol said. "Wear the other tie."

Uncle Dan put the nice tie on and gently handed the monkeyvomit tie to Aunt Carol.

"Take care of this, please. You made it for me, and so it will always be my favorite tie."

Aunt Carol gave me a threatening glance. I obviously wasn't supposed to reveal who had actually made the tie. I gave her a **thumbs-up** to indicate that I was in on this crime with her.

When an adult gives you THIS LOOK

just go along with it.

It's Thursday, so they were testing a new menu item at lunch today. They called it **Tropical Surprise**.

Of course it was totally unappetizing, but mostly I didn't feel like eating because I was too busy swallowing my pride to confess to Isabella.

"**I lost the bet**," I said, "but I was only mean because it was the nicest thing I could do. When you say something mean to be nice, it should count as niceness," I said.

"Jelly beans should count as beans," Isabella said with a wicked grin. "But add them to your mom's chili and watch what happens."

"So I'm getting the dare, huh?" I said.

"Oh, yes," she said happily. "**Oh yes yes yes yes yes yes.**"

"One for me, too," Angeline said. "I lost, too."

"No, she didn't," I said.

"I did, Jamie. It was all part of the same conversation. You said one tie was ugly, I said one was beautiful. I also lost."

Isabella began to visibly shake, and I realized why. After years of not getting to play Dare or Worse Dare with anyone, now she was getting to play it with **TWO PEOPLE** all at once.

She was so overwhelmed with joy that she actually **threw up** right there on the cafeteria floor, which grossed out everybody pretty badly except me.

"Hey, I have a couple of shirts that would go with that," I said.

FRIDAY 27

Dear Dumb Diary,

    We had our final debates in social studies today. Isabella was absent, and I know why. It wasn't because she still felt sick. It was because she wanted **all day** to focus on our dares. Heck, it wouldn't surprise me if she had even made herself throw up so that she could stay home today. Isabella can will herself to perform just about any bodily function at any moment, including sweat. **It's a talent.**

    Since Isabella wasn't there, Dicky suggested that he just debate himself, because he had been working so closely with Isabella that he knew **exactly** what she would say. Besides, he often talked to himself in the shower.

    Before Dicky began to describe the shower conversations — and he was preparing to — Mr. Smith said that Dicky had won by forfeit so he got to pick the subject for the next pair of debaters: me and Angeline.

SERIOUSLY, DICKY KEEP SHOWER CONVERSATIONS TO YOURSELF

EDEO

"Very well," Dicky said in his most dignified lisp. "I challenge both of thee to tell us why the **OTHER ONE** is a better person."

Mr. Smith's eyes widened.

"Each debater must say why the other is better," he said quietly, as if he was saying some sort of magic spell. "It means that if you lose, you win. . . ."

Angeline went first.

"I can't tell you how jealous I am of Jamie," she said, and I think I **swallowed my gum**. "She's really great at writing and drawing. She's a super-loyal best friend to Isabella, and she admits when she loses a bet. She's funny, and smart, and a good dancer, and she was right and I was wrong about the Hotdog Fiesta.

"She's actually right about a lot of things, if you give her some time to figure them out. I couldn't have a better cousin, although I'm pretty sure we're not really cousins. Without a doubt, she's a **better person** than I am."

For a moment I didn't know what to say.

And for the moment after that, I still didn't.

Somewhere around the fourth or fifth moment, I knew, and I stood up to speak.

"I used to be **jealous** of Angeline because she's beautiful. She's so beautiful that it actually hurts my feelings to look at her face. For years, I've been hoping that she would turn out to be really mean or really selfish or really stupid, or that the beautiful would just fall off her like when my parakeet molted from a beautiful bird to a living, breathing McNugget.

"But she hasn't. Angeline is really and truly nice, but not just because she was born that way. Nobody is born that nice. Bunnies aren't born that nice. Angeline works at being nice. That doesn't mean it isn't genuine. Work **is** genuine. Believe me, I tried it.

"In fact, what you just naturally are isn't really much to be proud of. It's the things you work at, the things you do **on purpose**, that are accomplishments.

"Angeline is always a good friend to me even though I don't deserve it, and I have a feeling that if I was ever locked away in jail, Isabella might try to break me out with dynamite, but Angeline would be able to explain to the warden why I deserved to be released.

"I used to be jealous of Angeline because she's beautiful. Now I realize that there is **so much more** to be jealous of."

It's almost impossible to hug a friend in front of a class full of people. But Angeline comes in pretty fast for a hug, and I was hugged before I knew what hit me.

As I stood there, being strangled badly by Angeline, I realized where she was getting her meanness: Angeline feels jealous. Not of hair, or beauty — she's jealous of the things she thinks she doesn't have. It was just as hard for Angeline to say those things about me as it was for me to say them about her.

Hudson turned to Mr. Smith and asked him who won, but he was still puzzling over the way Dicky had set up the debate.

"How did you ever come up with something so **fiendish**?" he asked Dicky, who just shrugged and stuck his thumb in his belly button.

We Love you Dicky

But Keep your thumb out of places pLz

CRAM

When I got home, I told Mom that Uncle Dan **really** liked the tie, and that Aunt Carol told him that she made it.

"It meant a lot to Uncle Dan. He said it's his favorite tie in the world."

Mom's chin wrinkled, and she touched one hand lightly over her heart.

"So I think you'd better not make any of your homemade clothing items for a while," I went on. "At least until he forgets about it. We don't want to spoil things for Aunt Carol." Mom nodded in agreement.

I looked at Dad and silently mouthed the words, "Now **you** owe **me**, and I want Chinese food."

"I got the promotion," he said with a grin. "Who wants Chinese food?"

The more MOVED a Mom is, the more closely her chin resembles an elephant's butt

SATURDAY 28

Dear Dumb Diary,

Today, Angeline and I stood before Isabella to meet our fates. She had dressed all in black, like some kind of executioner, and she made a big production of **slooooowly** putting her little notebook on the table and looking at us over her glasses.

"I suppose you two know what I have in this little notebook," she said in a low, sinister tone of voice.

"Our dares?" Angeline said.

"Indeed," Isabella confirmed. It was probably the first time she had ever used that word. "But first, a formality. **DARE** or **WORSE DARE?**" she asked.

"Dare," we said in unison.

"Are you sure?" she said. "The Worse Dares look pretty good to me. I don't want to give anything away, but one of them involves a bucket of fish heads."

"Dare," we repeated.

"Very well," Isabella said as dramatically as she could. She opened her notebook.

"As different as the two of you are, you might find it interesting that my careful thinking has led me to conclude that the very best dare for you both is the **Exact Same Dare.**"

Isabella paused as if she was waiting for thunder.

"Oh, get on with it," Angeline said.

"Angeline and Jamie, I dare the two of you to . . ."

pretty sure the worse dares involved a knife, fork, and bib, too

". . . say what the best things are about the other one!" she proclaimed in a booming voice. She folded her arms, leaned back, and smiled.

"You're joking, right?" I said, and Angeline started to snicker.

"**NO JOKE.** This is it. You have agreed to this, and this is the dare you must accept. I've given this a lot of careful thought, Angeline. You're sweet, but you know that you'll never be good at the things Jamie's good at, and that's where your weakness is. I've figured you out, Angeline. Your flaw is jealousy."

"You're right," Angeline said, "I am jealous." And she repeated, word-for-word, what she had said about me yesterday. And then I did the same.

Isabella's smile turned into a look of puzzlement, and then anger.

"Why isn't this just destroying you???" she demanded.

We told her about the debate, and how Dicky already gave this exact same challenge. We had said it all before.

Isabella kicked over her chair and shook her fist at the sky.

"**DICKY!!!!!!**"

Turns out that Isabella had been trying dare ideas on Dicky all along during their debate practice, without ever telling him what they were really for. Because Dicky doesn't have a mean bone in his body, he just happened to like the sound of this one, because he figured what could ever possibly be wrong about saying **nice things**?

I actually felt a little bad for Isabella. She just wanted to have one more go at a little game that she had innocently played as a child with savage and inhuman cruelty.

I **almost** let her give me another dare, but I had heard something about fish heads.

There's nothing sadder than a pouting evil genius

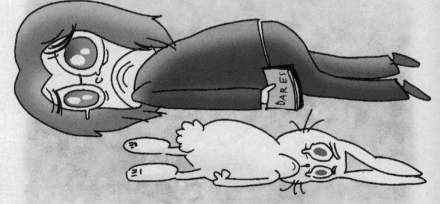

Pouting Bunnies come close, Dude. pretty close

Dear Dumb Diary,

I talked to Isabella today. She was so enraged yesterday that she made Dicky play Dare or Worse Dare with her.

She had not had much time to prepare, so she meanly dared him to wear her monkeyvomit hat all day. **And he did.**

He even photographed himself wearing it with some clown makeup on, and posted it on the Student Awareness Committee blog as the logo.

It got more than **200 likes**, way more than anything any of us had ever posted.

It's weird: When Dicky made us give each other compliments, it was to be nice, and when Isabella made us do the same thing, it was to be mean. The **exact same thing** could be nice and mean at the same time.

Like telling somebody that you love the awful shirt they made you.

Like letting somebody know the tie they're wearing is a nightmare.

Like Angeline and me. We're nice and mean at the same time.

Like antibiotics and probiotics.

Things just aren't black and white.

Life is like a monkeyvomit hat, Dumb Diary. It can be bad one minute, and good the next, but most often, it's probably both at the exact same time, and you won't always know which is which. **You can bet on that.**

Thanks for listening, Dumb Diary,

Jamie Kelly

How Do You REALLY Feel?

for example, I am NORMAL.

But Angeline is ABNORMAL.

And Isabella is ABNORMALLER.

Jamie, Angeline, and Isabella each have their own way of seeing the world. Who are you most like? Answer the questions below to find out — and be honest!

1.) What's your favorite season?
   a. Summer! I love warm days. And kind of warm days. And sunshine. And pool parties. And lemonade. And . . .
   b. The deep, dark freeze of winter.
   c. Spring, I guess. (Except for the rain. And the mud.)

2.) When you play Truth or Dare, you usually choose:
   a. Truth — I have nothing to hide!
   b. Neither — I'm too busy daring everyone else.
   c. Dare — I just prepare myself for the worst.

3.) If your mom made you a super-ugly monkeyvomit shirt, what would you do?
   a. Wear it happily — she put a lot of time and effort into it!
   b. Wear it immediately — to play tackle football in the mud (and hope that it gets completely destroyed . . . along with my opponent).
   c. Wear it only until I'm out of her sight — as long as no one else can see me.

4.) You hear that the cafeteria is serving up a new recipe for lunch. What's your first thought?
   a. Ooh, yummy! I can't wait to try it!
   b. I wonder how many people will get food poisoning.
   c. It can't be worse than all the other gross stuff they serve . . . can it?

5.) You have the flu. You can't help thinking:
   a. It's nice to get some extra rest, and chicken soup is delicious!
   b. There must be a way to strengthen the germs and then pass them to my mean older brothers.
   c. It figures. I'm missing out on so much while I'm stuck at home!

6.) What's your favorite food?
   a. Anything sweet!
   b. Shish kebobs, fondue . . . anything on a sharp skewer.
   c. Pizza. Unless it has mushrooms. Or too many gross veggies. Or too much cheese.

7.) A friend leaves a box of chocolates in your locker. What do you do?
   a. Run to find her immediately, give her a big hug, and thank her 20 times.
   b. Test each chocolate for poison (you never know), and then eat them all at once so I don't have to share with anyone.
   c. Wonder what she did wrong. Why else would she give me a gift out of the blue? It seems suspicious.

8.) Your dad is planning to wear the world's ugliest sweater to have his work portrait taken. What do you do?

a. Pick out something different, and sweetly suggest that it would look even better than the sweater.

b. Let him wear it, and cackle every time you see the photo.

c. Give him a long speech about how hideously ugly and awful the sweater is, and how he should be embarrassed to even own it.

If you answered . . .

Mostly As: Like Angeline, you always look on the sunny side! People may find your positive outlook annoyingly chipper, but you don't notice. You're too busy smiling and tickling puppies and singing to unicorns.

Mostly Bs: Like Isabella, you have your own unique way of seeing the world, where "unique" is a nice way of saying "slightly terrifying." You may or may not have mean older brothers to blame for this, but either way, you should probably scale it back a little.

Mostly Cs: Like Jamie, you can be a bit negative sometimes — but you prefer to think of yourself as realistic. Except when it comes to koalas. There is nothing negative about koalas.

Designed By You!

If Dicky Flartsnutt can design an awesome logo, so can you! Try your hand at drawing something for these different organizations:

The Student Awareness Committee

Clown-Haters Anonymous

The Society for Protection Against Those Who Are
Effortlessly Beautiful

Glittermaniacs

The Association for the Appreciation of Koala
Fuzziness

HEY! WHATEVER YOU DO, DON'T LOOK FOR JAMIE KELLY'S NEXT **TOP SECRET** DIARY....

DEAR DUMB DIARY YEAR TWO #6

Turn the page for a super-secret sneak peek. . . .

DEAR DUMB DIARY,

CAN'T GET ENOUGH OF JAMIE KELLY?
CHECK OUT HER OTHER DEAR DUMB DIARY BOOKS!

YEAR TWO: #1: School. Hasn't This Gone On Long Enough?

YEAR TWO: #2: The Super-Nice are Super-Annoying

YEAR TWO: #3: Nobody's Perfect. I'm As Close As It Gets.

YEAR TWO: #4: What I Don't Know Might Hurt Me

WWW.SCHOLASTIC.COM/DEARDUMBDIARY

#1: Let's Pretend This Never Happened

#2: My Pants Are Haunted!

#3: Am I the Princess or the Frog?

#4: Never Do Anything, Ever

#5: Can Adults Become Human?

#6: The Problem With Here Is That It's Where I'm From

#7: Never Underestimate Your Dumbness

#8: It's Not My Fault I Know Everything

#9: That's What Friends Aren't For

#10: The Worst Things In Life Are Also Free

#11: Okay, So Maybe I Do Have Superpowers

#12: Me! (Just Like You, Only Better)

Our Dumb Diary: A Journal to Share

Totally Not Boring School Planner

Four girls, one charm bracelet, and a little bit of luck . . .

Charmed Life
Caitlin's Lucky Charm
LISA SCHROEDER
SCHOLASTIC

Charmed Life
Mia's Golden Bird
LISA SCHROEDER
SCHOLASTIC

Charmed Life
Libby's Sweet Surprise
LISA SCHROEDER
SCHOLASTIC

Charmed Life
Hannah's Bright Star
LISA SCHROEDER
SCHOLASTIC

From the author of *It's Raining Cupcakes* comes a charming series about how anything is possible when you have great friends!

Some guys just can't win...but Danny never stops trying!

Graphic novels by #1 *New York Times* bestselling author
Raina Telgemeier

This is the true story of how Raina severely injured her two front teeth when she was in the sixth grade, and the dental drama – on top of boy confusion, a major earthquake, and friends who turn out to be not so friendly – that followed!

Callie is the set designer for her middle school's spring musical, and is determined to create a set worthy of Broadway. But between the onstage AND offstage drama that occurs once the actors are chosen, it's going to be a long way until opening night!

Confectionately Yours

Don't miss all the books in this delicious series!

About Jim Benton

Jim Benton is not a middle-school girl, but do not hold that against him. He has managed to make a living out of being funny, anyway.

He is the creator of many licensed properties, some for big kids, some for little kids, and some for grown-ups who, frankly, are probably behaving like little kids.

You may already know his properties: It's Happy Bunny™ or Catwad™, and of course you already know about Dear Dumb Diary.

He's created a kids' TV series, designed clothing, and written books.

Jim Benton lives in Michigan with his spectacular wife and kids. They do not have a dog, and they especially do not have a vengeful beagle. This is his first series for Scholastic.

Jamie Kelly has no idea that Jim Benton, or you, or anybody is reading her diaries. So, please, please, please don't tell her.